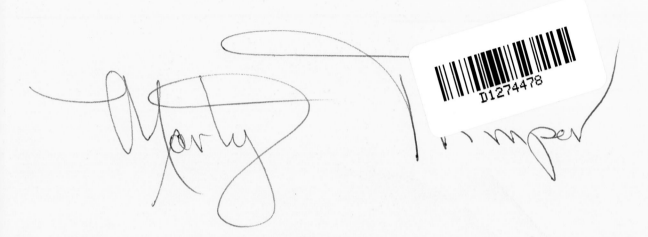

HERMIONE

HERMIONE IN TRIMPER'S AMUSEMENT PARK IN OCEAN CITY, MARYLAND
Copyright © 2006 Marty Trimper
All rights reserved.

Published by Marty Trimper
1530 Teal Drive, Ocean City, MD 21842
(410) 289-8207 • FAX (410) 289-8207
E-mail: info@martytrimper.com
Web Site: www.martytrimper.com
Illustrated by Amy Holloway
Edited by Marty Trimper
Printed by BookMasters, Inc., Mansfield, OH

ISBN: 0-9785979-0-7

Library of Congress Control Number: 2006903915

HERMIONE

in Trimper's Amusement Park

Ocean City, Maryland

Written by
MARTY TRIMPER

Illustrated by
AMY HOLLOWAY

You may travel to areas of the United States other than Ocean City, Maryland, certainly to Europe or to other parts of the world and find wonderful antiques far older than the Trimper's 1902 carousel. It would be difficult, though, to find one more loved and cherished and which has endured the hands of millions of children as they sit astride their favorite animal. As of this writing the Trimper's treasured "family heirloom" is in its 104th year of continuous operation.

Patrons of the amusement park, from the youngest child to the oldest great-grandparent, all have stories to tell and most with pictures to show of repeat visits to ride this menagerie of 48 animals. And, of course, to take advantage of the many other amusement rides in Trimper's Park—from the Frog Hopper to whirling Teacups to the mysteries of the Pirate's Cove and the Haunted House.

While mention of the Haunted House brings us to the subject of this book: Hermione Hippopotamus, who has taken up residence in a secret room . . .

AUTHOR'S NOTE—HERMIONE, SHIPWRECKED! IN OCEAN CITY, MARYLAND, is the first book in this Hermione Hippopotamus series.

Dedicated to
our families and friends
who encouraged us
in writing our stories and
in painting our pictures
to preserve
"What Fun Is All About"—
TRIMPER'S AMUSEMENT PARK,
Originating in 1890

ermione Hippopotamus lived in Trimper's Amusement Park but no one else was ever quite sure. You see she did not live there in a cage like a circus animal but had a secret hiding place during the day and at night she slipped out to explore and enjoy the Park. Somehow Hermione knew that if grownups caught her she would be caged or taken away, perhaps to a zoo.

She did not know what a "zoo" was except for hearing that many animals were kept in such a place. Her parents had told her that the Big Game people had come one year and captured her Uncle Joe Smith and Aunt Aruska. They had even heard the Big Game people say they were shipping them to the Smithsonian Zoo in Washington, DC.

Hermione wished she had listened to her parents when they had told her not to stray away from them. They had cautioned that the same thing that had happened to Uncle Joe and Aunt Aruska could happen to her.

The warning of her parents faded and when Hermione was five years old she had ventured outside the game preserve and was captured. Her cage was placed on the deck of a huge container ship bound for zoos in America. She was saved from at least that fate by the terrible storm that had ripped open her cage, swept her overboard and washed her ashore onto Ocean City's beach.

On that dark and rain-drenched night she had trudged her way across the beach to the boardwalk and found shelter in a long-forgotten secret room of Trimper's Haunted House.

Hermione's first desire was to be back in East Africa with her parents but, knowing that was not possible, she was still happy and never thought about wanting to live anywhere else. She loved Trimper's Amusement Park with all the thousands of children who visited in the summer.

Hermione could look through the knotholes in her secret room at the back of the Haunted House and see the children riding. She danced to the music from the rides and smiled at the squeals of excitement from the children and delighted laughter of the adults.

Hermione wished she could join the children on the rides. Her favorites were the Balloons as they swung round and round with their colorful lights and then she liked the children's roller coaster, too.

Oh, no—she did not mean the great big Tidal Wave roller coaster that went so very high and even turned its riders upside down!

Nor would Hermione go near the Pirate Ship: It reminded her too much of being caught and forced into a cage. Sometimes she still had bad dreams of the turbulent journey she had had on that ship.

When the Park closed at night Hermione would push against the loose board that allowed her to come and go from her secret room. She took care that the security guard was not around and then she would come dancing out.

Hermione had such fun in the Park. Her four sturdy legs were an especially useful asset at the roly-poly exit to the Fun House.

Hermione had only tried the Mirror Maze once since it had soon thoroughly confused her with its myriad reflections. When she had started through it had been about 4 in the morning but already dawning light by the time she found her way out. Hermione was lucky not to have been seen by early bicyclists and joggers on their way to the boardwalk.

Amazingly, they were too engrossed in getting their exercise to pay attention to the "closed" attraction and no one saw her as she scampered back to her room.

The Bumper Boats were the most relaxing for Hermione. She would scramble into the boat and it would drift and float and lazily spin about the pool. Memories of her African homeland lakes made her think what fun it would be to have bumper boats there.

Hermione wanted so much to ride the Frog Hopper, and Airplanes, the Tea Cups and the Merry Mixer

but had not yet found a way to turn them on and ride without being discovered.

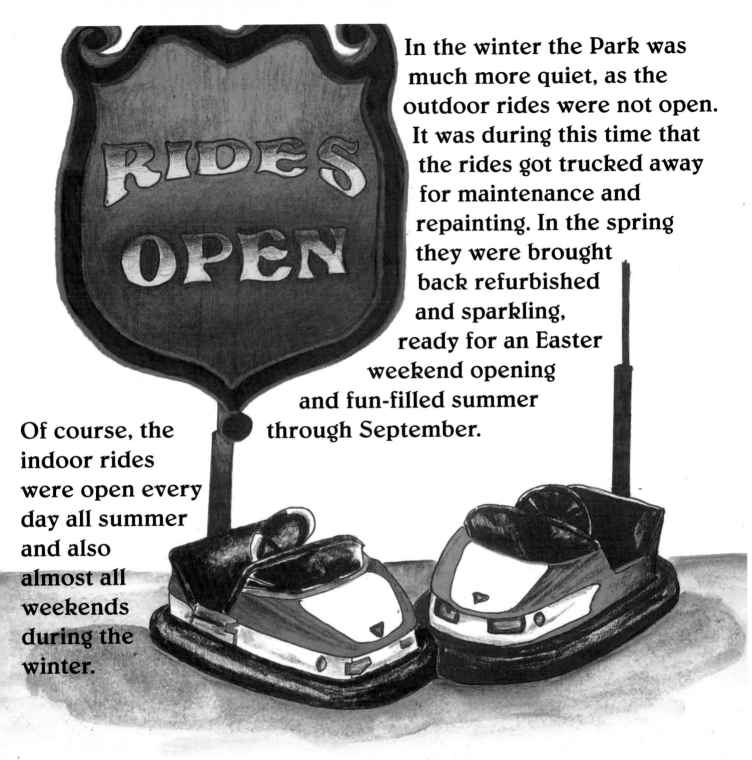

In the winter the Park was much more quiet, as the outdoor rides were not open. It was during this time that the rides got trucked away for maintenance and repainting. In the spring they were brought back refurbished and sparkling, ready for an Easter weekend opening and fun-filled summer through September.

Of course, the indoor rides were open every day all summer and also almost all weekends during the winter.

One adventurous night Ronnie, the security guard, just missed catching Hermione coming down the slide at the Raiders of the Lost Ark. She had climbed the steps OK but walking across the bridge in the netting was pretty tricky. Several times her four feet got caught all at once, spilling her in a heap.

Hermione knew Ronnie's schedule and had hurried to get down the slide before he was due to come by the Avalanche ride. But then he was almost to the Park gate and would surely see her! Fortunately, though, he had stopped to feed the kittens, bending over just outside the gate, and did not see Hermione skirting the shadows to get back to her secret room.

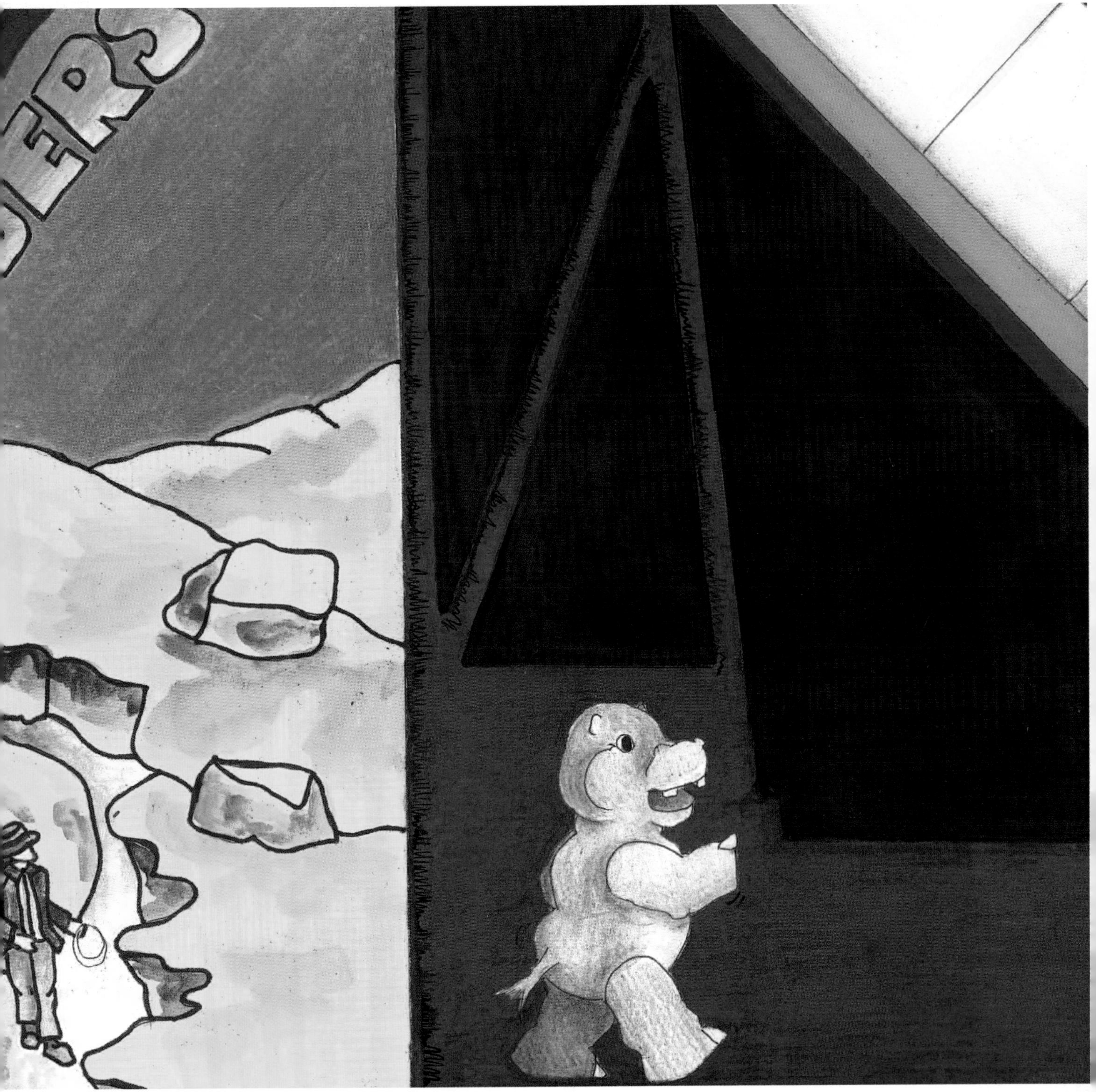

Among the indoor rides, Hermione loved the antique merry-go-round best. It made her think of Africa because the menagerie contained a zebra,

lion and tiger. But she also liked the others: there were many horses, plus a cat, dog, reindeer, frog and

rooster. She only wished that there had been a hippopotamus, too; still, she considered them company.

Hermione Hippopotamus was often hungry. Her diet in East Africa had been grasses and always readily available but here in Trimper's Amusement Park she had a tough time finding grass or greens of any kind.

When she had first arrived she had been afraid to venture very far from her secret room to search for food. Once she had gone just far enough to chew on the little rose bush planted near the Bulls Eye game—but had gotten sticky thorns in her mouth.

She was more brave now, though, and after the Park would close she would saunter over behind the Tidal Wave roller coaster to the fence that separated the Park from the street. Hedges which had been planted there were thick and handily hid her from view of any passersby. The diet of hedge leaves and grazing along a spare strip of grass was not the most nutritious but had quieted her hunger pangs.

One night as she munched her way along the fence she came by the train ride, looked up and across the street. What did she see but

a veritable paradise of grasses, vines and bushes of every description, even flowers and full-grown trees and the most wondrous of all: several ponds of water! There were also

paths leading through it all: Hermione had discovered Olde Towne Miniature Golf Course.

TRIMPER'S OLDE TOWNE GOLF

Immediately, Hermione wanted to trot over there. But here she was behind the high fence which completely surrounded the Park and the gates were chained. She eagerly followed the fence perimeter until she came to the fastened gate. She nudged a clamp but a loose chain still restrained it. Persistently she continued to push against it until she had wedged her head between the gate and the chain, then found the gate would open just enough for her to push her body through.

She looked quickly up and down the street and toward the boardwalk to make sure no one was about, then Hermione trotted swiftly across to the miniature golf course.

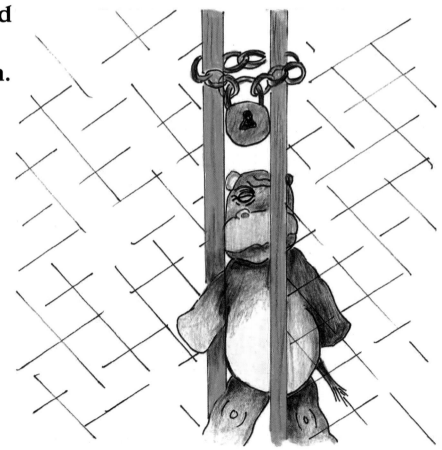

Yes. Here was a virtual feast and plenty of water to drink and in which to bathe. Hermione sampled first one bush and then another and digested copious mouthfuls of ivy vines, and for dessert she even sampled the flowers. She waded in the ponds and drank so much that she was almost water-logged. All the greenery and ponds and waterfalls made Hermione think of her home in East Africa and she suddenly felt lonely and missed her parents and other hippopotamus playmates.

But there was little time to feel homesick. As dawn began to break over the ocean, Hermione saw a small grey pickup truck pull into the golf course parking lot. A door slammed and then a cheery whistle was heard; it was Jack, who used to manage the golf course every day.

Now, however, Jack was the curator of the Wheels of Yesterday Antique and Classic Car Museum. And although he loved his new job, he still retained a fondness for the golf course and had just stopped by to inspect a new water pump.

Hermione was panic-stricken. She had stayed far too long in the golf course eating and playing in the water. Now she would be caught! She stood rigid in the pond, not knowing what to do.

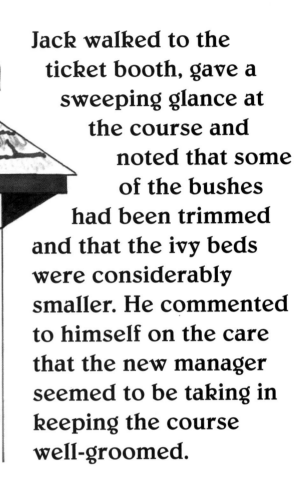

Jack walked to the ticket booth, gave a sweeping glance at the course and noted that some of the bushes had been trimmed and that the ivy beds were considerably smaller. He commented to himself on the care that the new manager seemed to be taking in keeping the course well-groomed.

Then Jack spoke aloud to himself, "Why look there: Granville has added a rhinoceros to the pond. I didn't know he was going to do that." Hermione had heard what Jack said and although she was incensed by what Jack had called her, she was scared too stiff to move.

Almost at once Jack realized his mistake because he added, "No, it cannot be a rhinoceros because for one thing it doesn't have a horn in the middle of its nose; instead, it must be a hippopotamus." He glanced at his watch, noting that if he didn't hurry he would be late for his job at the Museum. So Jack had not ventured nearer to the motionless Hermione for a closer look at the "new addition." There was then a shuddering sigh of relief from Hermione as Jack, having gotten in his truck, whisked away down the street.

Immediately Hermione had climbed from the pool, looked quickly in all directions, saw no one and returned to the fence. Once again, she wedged her way between the chain and gate and had just reached her secret room as the first of the Park's maintenance crew arrived to sweep and clean the Park.

Because the carousel was her favorite of everything in the Park, Hermione had spent much of her time looking to see what made it run. Then one night when she ventured out after the Park closed, and had made sure Ronnie the security guard was busy checking out the Inlet Lodge Motel or over by Marty's Playland, Hermione had found the switch that turned on the carousel with its music!

From then on, once assured she was the only one in the building, Hermione would push the switch, jump on the carousel and ride in one of the big rocking chairs, swaying and humming to the music.

So think twice if you're ever on the Boardwalk late at night and you hear the lilting sounds of the carousel's calliope . . .

To be continued in Book Three:

The Further Adventures of

HERMIONE AND HER BUCKEROO ADVENTURE

(that includes a wild ride to Frontier Town and Buckeroo Park,
and a trip to Assateague State and National Seashore Parks)

* * *

Book One of The "Hermione" Series is

Available at Ocean City Book Stores,

Museum Gift Stores and Shops

in addition to other locations.

Ask for:

HERMIONE, SHIPWRECKED! IN OCEAN CITY, MARYLAND